THE TALE OF THE MAGIC SNOWFALL

GINA C. PATE

outskirts
press

Outskirts Press, Inc.
http://www.outskirtspress.com

Paperback ISBN: 978-1-9772-5371-2
Hardback ISBN: 978-1-9772-5935-6

Illustrations by Richa Kinra © 2023 Gina C Pate. All rights reserved - used with permission.

Outskirts Press and the "OP" logo are trademarks belonging to Outskirts Press, Inc.

PRINTED IN THE UNITED STATES OF AMERICA

This book is dedicated to my grandmother, Cristina Brusco, the greatest storyteller of my childhood. Thank you, Grandma, for entertaining me with a good story at a moment's notice.

Chapter 1

FLUFF ARRIVES

"What a beautiful place," Fluff exclaimed, "But where is everyone? There must be another cloud here somewhere." Fluff looked from east to west, as well as way up above him, and saw nothing but blue skies. "It's an especially sunny day," he said. "I'll just stay put and enjoy my new home until the others come along." Fluff took time to enjoy his surroundings. The village below was everything you would expect of a small town in the Northeast: mountains, rolling hills, streams and valleys. It was beautiful with the last tinges of autumn color, and he was just in time to be part of the winter months.

Fluff was overjoyed to have finally made it to the skies over this little town. His placement had not been easy, mostly because he was confused about just what type of weather he wanted to be a part of. You see, Fluff was a cumulous cloud, and a very large and fluffy one at that. He had many curving arches making up his overall egg-shape. He was the pride and joy of the cloud nursery and with so much enthusiasm from the cloud academy, he was expected to play an excellent part in world weather. Any town would be lucky to have him in the skies above.

After much trial and error, he finally realized he wanted to grace the earth below with a beautiful snowfall. No tornados or hurricanes for him. Instead of causing damage, he wanted to create beauty. He was sure of that now. Just beautiful snowflakes carpeting the earth below in beautiful white fluffiness. It made him so happy to think of all the townspeople enjoying nature. He finally arrived in the northeast, where he could take part in all four seasons and where winters are cold and more importantly, snowy!

"Oh, hi there. Fluff, right? My name is Buffy, but everyone calls me Buff for short."

Fluff glimpsed before him a neat and petite cloud full of white tufts, and with slight gray edging. She wasn't as strikingly large as himself, but he could see she was spirited, with a take-charge personality.

"Yes, Fluff. That's me. How do you know my name?"

"You are famous among the cloud cover. All the neighboring clouds are talking about you! Welcome to the skies over the town of Silver Slopes. We're all happy to have you on our team."

Fluff's excitement soared so high, his vapor condensed into fluffier tufts and dense spiraling puffs. He became whiter but with a tinge of red around his puffy cheeks due to his embarrassment.

Buff was a little confused and concerned. "Are you alright, Fluff? No need to get nervous. Should I be calling in the emergency support clouds?"

"No need. I am just fine," answered Fluff, trying to control the pace of his vaporizing. "Let me just catch my breath. I hope I didn't startle you. I'm just so happy to be here! This happens to me whenever I'm overjoyed and a little more than enthusiastic." Fluff paused to take a calming breath. "Well, I guess it also happens when I am nervous or afraid, but I may look a little different in that case. Now that I think of it, I'm not really sure if I do look different when I am worried. Anyway, you see, I can't wait to get to work. This winter is going to be glorious!"

"Glorious?"

Fluff didn't even hear the question. He continued with zeal. "I loved creating snowflakes in my *Winter Wonderland* class. I got an A in that class by the way, but I shouldn't be boastful. Oh, those beautiful flakes! It makes my vapor even mistier just thinking about them. I know things can be more unexpected in nature, but I am so excited to try! Sorry again. I'm doing so much talking."

"That's okay. You are definitely hyped-up. Just the kind of cloud we need here."

"It's all so exciting. I can almost feel my vapor getting colder and ready to form beautiful snowflakes. So tell me about snowfalls past, what was last winter like? Did we have any fantastic blizzards?"

Ignoring that question, Buff nervously avoided eye contact with Fluff. She was relieved to have such an impressive cloud with her in the sky. This winter should be successfully snowy. No need to sadden this newcomer with too many details about the past. Fluff was just what was needed to bring about the snowfall everyone had been waiting for. There shouldn't be anything holding them back now. Buff shifted his attention to the neighboring clouds. "Let me introduce you to our support team: Hazel, Drizzle and Foggy. We all work together here."

Fluff made acquaintance with his new friends and enjoyed a warm welcome. "Wow, you guys are great-looking support clouds. We can create some impressive snowfalls."

"Yes, I guess we could create a snowfall," responded Hazel drearily. She was a grayish cloud with tinges of purple haze.

"We should have some success now that you're here. I knew Mother Nature was working on solving our problem," added Drizzle, a cloud with a little more moisture than most.

"Problem? What problem?" asked Fluff.

"The problem of a snowfall," added Foggy, while his murk continually separated and floated away.

Buff quickly sought to steer everyone away from this topic. "Now is not the time for details," she said. "Let's give Fluff a chance to settle in and get familiar with his surroundings. We have many snowfalls ahead of us."

Fluff was not sure what he was hearing from these clouds, but he was a little concerned with the "no snowfall" comment from Foggy. Maybe he was just confused. Fog could do that to a cloud, especially with all the heavy mist. It can be very distracting.

"Come everyone, let's get Fluff familiar with Silver Slopes. It's a great little town," said Buff as positively as she could.

"Yes, see where the ski slopes used to be?" added Hazel. "They were quite striking from this vantage point."

"You mean, they used to be last winter?" asked Fluff, his voice trembling. His concern was growing by the minute.

"Well, maybe not last winter. Or maybe, not the one before either. I'm not sure what winter that was," said Hazel. "Do you remember, Foggy?"

"Now why would you ask me, Hazel? You know how my memory can be. That's how I got my name."

Drizzle added to this discussion with certainty. "It was about seven years ago. I remember because that was when I became part of this cloud cover. It was a beautiful year for snow, even though my contribution was a little slushy. It was understandable though; I was just starting out. Not so much snow since then."

"The last snowfall was seven years ago!" exclaimed Fluff in horror. "Why hasn't it snowed since then? That's terrible news!"

Buff realized she could no longer keep the situation under wraps. "We have had a bit of a dry spell in the winter months. We're not sure why, but we are hoping things will change with you on our team. After all, as you said, you did get an A in your

THE TALE OF THE MAGIC SNOWFALL

Winter Wonderland class. Things should be looking a lot frostier from now on."

"But I'm not sure how to fix this problem."

"Maybe our snowflakes were not as big as they should have been. I'm sure you can help with that."

"Maybe they had too much moisture," added Drizzle. "Mine were always a little too wet."

"Or maybe they just weren't energetic enough," said Foggy in his usual sleepy drawl. "You probably can help me figure out that low-energy issue."

"We do have some hurdles to overcome," said Buff. "But I know you'll be able to help us, Fluff. After all, you are now in charge of the sky over Silver Slopes. We're all happy to follow your lead."

Fluff looked from one cloud to the other in disbelief while his excitement and his vapor deflated. "I'm in charge? I think we're in trouble."

Chapter 2

MIKEY'S WISH

As the sunlight started dimming and the days became shorter, everyone in the little village of Silver Slopes, was preparing for the winter months. The firewood was neatly stacked in the sheds, the gardens had long finished supplying their harvest, the berries had all been made into jam, and the herbs were found hanging from the rafters in the barns. Villagers looked with hope to the sky to welcome those first few snowflakes.

Silver Slopes was a perfect place in which to enjoy the winter months. In fact, visitors have long come from far and wide to enjoy all the winter activities the village had to offer. Mountain trails swerved around glistening ponds and bluish green spruce trees. Red holly berries sparkled, frozen against the deep green leaves. The fireplaces in every home burned bright and comforting. There was something for everyone: skiers, snowboarders, skaters, and folks snuggled up in sleighs.

The problem was, it had been years since they had a beautiful white blanket of snow. The children dreamed of sleighs and snowmen, but only knew of these things in their imaginations.

Would they ever get to take that sleigh out for a ride in the brisk night air? They could only hope.

There was one special boy in town, excited about that first magical snowfall, even though those around him were doubtful. Mikey was a sandy-haired boy, full of energy, with a heart-shaped face and eyes glimmering with curiosity. He asked endless questions as he watched his grandfather, Jim, putting the last of the gardening tools in the barn. Whenever you saw Jim Doyle working outdoors, Mikey was sure to be right there with him.

Jim didn't mind. He loved working with his grandson, teaching him all about nature and small-town life. He wanted his grandson to grow up with a love and respect for the earth and the simple life. There wasn't anything more satisfying than planting your garden and caring for the vegetables as they grew and finally ripened. His rough hands were evidence of the work he did throughout the year. Jim was often seen in his yard wearing his black and red plaid jacket. He was a tall man, slender in build, with gray hair, kind eyes and a loving heart.

"Grandpa, do you think it will snow soon?" asked Mikey. "I really want to go sledding with you."

"Maybe we'll see some snow this winter," his grandfather answered, trying to keep a smile on his face and a positive tone to his voice. He knew how much Mikey wanted snow. His parents had left him in the care of his grandparents for the winter months. They were working at a ski resort in Silver Slopes, but since the town had not enjoyed snow in many years, they made the difficult decision to work far away from their hometown. They had to go where the snow was falling.

"I know it's going to happen soon," said Mikey. "It's getting really cold and cloudy. And it's going to be awesome. There are so many fun things we can do in the snow. We can build a snowman and even have a snowball fight. Don't you think it will snow soon?"

"I think we're due a snowy winter. Let's hope for a good one this year."

"I am more than hoping. I'm wishing for snow. Wishing is a little more than hoping."

"They say the weather has been changing everywhere. It does feel cold enough, though. I'm going to wish right along with you," answered Jim. "I think I'm done with my work for today. Let's go see your grandmother. I'll bet she has something delicious in the oven for dinner." With that, he guided Mikey to the house with a loving pat on the back.

When they entered the house, Mikey and his grandfather were greeted by the comforting aroma of simmering stew on the stove and warming bread in the oven. Grandma Lucy was where she could usually be found: that is in the kitchen. She was always baking or cooking, hair pulled up in a bun with loose graying strands framing her round face. She was a generous soul, always looking for opportunities to feed someone. Her loving smile reached from ear to ear. "Hi, you two." She busied herself with bowls of stew while Grandpa and Mikey washed and dried their hands in the kitchen sink. "Are you ready to get something warm to eat?" She took the bread from the oven and cut a generous slice for each of them. "Here you go, Mikey. Sit here next to your grandfather and dig in."

"Grandma, it looks like it might snow tonight," Mikey said enthusiastically as he chewed a big bite of bread.

"Is that so?" Lucy said, trying to hide the doubt in her voice. "Eat your stew before it gets cold and don't talk while you are chewing. When you're done, we can play checkers. You love trying to beat me at checkers."

"I mean it, Grandma. It could happen this very night. We can wake up tomorrow and see really deep snow."

"From your lips to God's ears. We certainly could use it. The store owners in town are saying their prayers along with you. I know your mom and dad are hoping to come back to work in their hometown, too." Lucy's heart ached while she answered her grandson. She knew how much the boy missed his parents.

"I am wishing for snow really hard and it's going to be awesome. Maybe even better than awesome. It's going to be spectacular!"

"Yes, snow would be spectacular. Finish your dinner and then we can give your mom and dad a call. They will want to know how much your grandfather is teaching you about harvesting the vegetables and getting ready for the winter."

Lucy peered into the pot, and realized she'd made much more stew than they need. "I think I will bring some of this stew to Mrs. Downing next door. I'll just put some aside for her and bring it over in the morning."

"I don't know why you bother with that woman," said Jim. "She is never grateful and she doesn't even like answering the door."

"I like to share what I have, and besides, there is so much stew it will probably go to waste."

"She is a loner, that one, and a little strange too. She's always mumbling something to herself. I don't know who she thinks she's talking to."

"I like her cat," said Mikey, breaking into the conversation. "I see her outside every day exploring and climbing the trees. She's a really awesome cat too."

Lucy went about packaging a generous helping for her neighbor. "She is all alone and can use some neighborly kindness," she said. "After all, kindness always touches the good in people."

Chapter 3

MRS. DOWNING

*U*nlike the neighborly townspeople of Silver Slopes, Mrs. Downing kept to herself. She was pleased with the current snowless conditions in their little town. She liked a peaceful and quiet life. Snow always led to confusion, noisy winter visitors and very dangerous situations.

Mrs. Downing was a short and stout woman, with plump cheeks and a long nose. She was stern, hardly ever making eye contact with anyone, and she'd never been seen with a smile on her face. Mrs. Downing was ever watchful of the comings and goings of those around her. Everything happening was her business and it was amazing how much you could learn about the townspeople from the safety of your living room window.

"My hopes must be realized again this year," said Mrs. Downing as she picked up her longhaired white cat, her faithful friend and prized possession. "No snow! No skiing! No sleigh riding! We need to get to spring without any trouble, right Bianca? Mother Nature has been very good to me these past winters. Everyone thinks I am a mean, old woman, but you know that isn't true, don't you Bianca?" she said, as she nuzzled her cat and placed her back on the floor. "What is all this hullabaloo about businesses and visitors? I like it just fine the way it is. After all, I have no need for snow and why should I be concerned with what everyone else in this town wants?"

There was a time Mrs. Downing enjoyed the snow along with others. She would never admit it now, but she liked seeing the trees covered in snow and sparkling in the moonlight.

All of that changed after that fateful winter day, years ago. Children had been playing happily in the snow all afternoon. Carelessly, a sled was left abandoned on the sidewalk at the end of the day. Overnight, as was typical, a fresh layer of snow fell and covered that sled so completely, it was easy to think it was only a pile of snow. Thinking just that, Mrs. Downing stepped on it and was immediately taken for a dangerous, downhill ride. She was such a sight that cars stopped on the street to witness that sled picking up speed while Mrs. Downing tottered back and forth, surfing down the hill. Children, not understanding that this was not of Mrs. Downing's choosing, delighted in the unusual sight of an adult taking such a daring ride. They laughed, cheered and clapped, as she shrieked and cried past them. She was finally stopped by a frozen holly bush on the corner.

The result of this mishap was a tangled mess of branches, red berries and Mrs. Downing. She wasn't hurt too badly, but her pride was hurt beyond repair. Her cheeks became inflamed as she gritted her teeth and stomped her way back home. It was not so much her fear as she took that wild ride, but anger and embarrassment. Her humiliation could only be described as a burning shame, so severe, it had never left her. In fact, ever since that day, the mere mention of snow brought an unusual redness to her face, and in Silver Slopes, snow was mentioned practically every day.

Chapter 4

SNOWFLAKES OR RAINDROPS

While the residents of Silver Slopes went about their daily lives, high up in the sky newly formed snowflakes danced throughout the misty cloud cover and grew stronger with each day. Fluff and Buff, along with the other clouds on their team, were proud of their success in forming such promising snowflakes. Fluff had been a wonderful addition to the cumulous cloud cover, teaching his new friends how to create the millions and millions of snowflakes needed for a beautiful snowfall. It wasn't the easiest of projects, what with Drizzle's tendency to water everything down and Foggy's lack of energy for anything but mist. Fluff was proud of his new cloud friends and what they had been able to create.

"These new snowflakes are beautiful, aren't they, Buff? They really sparkle and shine."

"They are beautiful. We have just the right amount of water for them. Even Drizzle has managed to make snowflakes that aren't so soggy and Foggy has learned to bring a little more energy to his flake-making. You have been a great team leader. It's so much fun to watch these snowflakes play while getting bigger and stronger."

"We really are the perfect playground for them, just the right amount of mist and cold," said Fluff. "All of their sides are so perfectly even; each one is a masterpiece, I think."

Buff chuckled at Fluff's pride and boastfulness. "We can't take all the credit. I think Mother Nature is the real reason for their beauty. She is the one that gives us what we need to grow crystals."

"Of course! Mother Nature is always in charge, but I think we'll have a very successful snowy winter this year. I am so confident we've solved the problem that has been hanging over Silver Slopes!"

"When are you going to tell him, Buff? You can't keep the story from him forever." Hazel turned to Fluff to break the sad news. "You see, it hasn't just been snowflake-making we have had issues with. Yes, you have helped improve our flake-making, but it hasn't been cold enough to release these flakes as flakes. Sometimes we release them, and they turn to raindrops. It has really been a terrible blow."

"Raindrops! In winter!" Fluff was flabbergasted. "We need to have a talk with Mother Nature about this. How can we do our job without her help? We need a little temperature change. That's all. She needs to give us a little cold air and there will be a perfect snowfall." Fluff was so overwhelmed with this news, his shape started to constrict and contort into odd-shaped peaks as he panted, releasing much of his vapor and shrinking in size.

Alarmed, Buff tried calming him down. "Fluff, you are going to completely disappear if you continue to work yourself up in this way. You're losing too much vapor. I'm sure we can find a way to get help."

As the clouds discussed their options and Fluff tried to calm down, the snowflakes, particularly, three of them, Crystal, Denny and Stella, danced, pranced and twirled from Buff to Fluff and back again. As they ignored the discussion of their uncertain fate, they twirled to the top of the clouds, floating downward, being carried by the wind, glistening while they played and laughing while they floated.

"This is one of the best days for floating," said Denny. "The wind is just perfect for cloud gliding."

"Be careful where you're floating," cried Crystal. "You might ruin my perfect six sides if you bump into me. You know I'm the most perfect of flakes and I want to stay that way."

"You're always too worried about how you look," answered Stella as she glided along. "I think all of us are beautiful without all the worry."

"You know I'm right, Stella. You know Denny can be too rough. We can't keep bumping into each other; we'll lose our perfect symmetry!"

"You two are ridiculous. Let's just have some fun. The more we play, the bigger we get," said Denny while soaring upward and spinning in place.

"We know, but we also need to be careful," said Crystal. "I want to be the most beautiful snowflake to fall to the ground ever. That can be in my future, if you would stop racing around me so out of control. Tell him, Stella."

"I think you two should stop bickering."

"That's what I mean," answered Denny. "I need to keep moving. You want to be the most beautiful snowflake, Crystal, but I am going to be the biggest snowflake to fall to the ground."

"Yeah, you will be big and missing most of your six sides. You'll be a forgotten flake, while I will be glistening all the way to the ground."

Stella couldn't help laughing at the thought of Denny's missing sides and Crystal glistening to the ground even though she had more serious things on her mind. "As much fun as you two are having, we have a problem to think about. We won't be going anywhere without the right temperature. We can twirl and prance all we want, but if it doesn't get colder soon, we won't be anything but a raindrop."

"A raindrop!" cried Crystal. "That would be horrible. What can we do about that? My dream is not to fall to the ground as a droplet of water. What about my glistening symmetry? That would be terrible. Is Stella telling the truth? Do we have to worry about becoming a raindrop?"

Buff and Fluff surround the flakes as Buff answered Crystal with as much comfort as she could. "I am sorry to say it could happen, and it's happened before. In recent years many beautiful flakes have turned to rain, but we still have hope in Mother Nature. Fluff plans on traveling to her castle and speaking with her. We'll do whatever we can to help bring about a snowfall and we promise you three will be a part of it."

"Me?" said a trembling Fluff. "I don't think I'm the one to talk with her. Just thinking about it makes my vapor thin with fear, and you know what might happen to me then. I could disappear altogether. *Someone* should have a talk with her, but *I* can't actually do it."

"But Fluff, you have the authority to represent all of us. You know you have that commanding presence."

"What does that mean exactly? I don't have a commanding presence. My presence is about to evaporate just thinking about it."

Buff, determined to convince Fluff, tried to appeal to his compassion. "Look at those beautiful snowflakes, Fluff. It would be a shame if we couldn't set them free."

"Oh, I know," answered Fluff reluctantly. He pictured the snowflakes gliding to the ground and blanketing everything in white. "They are beautiful." With renewed confidence he said, "I guess I'll do it. I do want to see those perfect snowflakes float to the ground. I'm sure she'll see our need and be happy to send a little cold our way. I'm sure she will, but I am not sure I know what to say."

"Just tell her about the beautiful snowflakes we have waiting to fall to the ground. Tell her how hard we have worked to improve our flake-making and how successful we've been. Ask her when we can expect to release all of them."

"You make it sound so simple, but I'm not sure this is really going to help," said Fluff, all the while knowing he had to accept his mission.

"You have to try, Fluff," begged Foggy. "I can't keep hold of these snowflakes much longer. I am getting a little tired of all this activity."

"Me too," added Hazel. "We did our part, now Mother Nature needs to do hers."

Chapter 5

READY FOR WINTER

*I*t seemed life in the clouds was not as carefree as some would imagine. While those active snowflakes dreamed of their journey to the ground, the clouds had trouble containing them.

In the meantime, life in Silver Slopes was as quiet as ever. The townspeople looked to the sky and wondered what the weather would bring this winter. Mr. John Parsons, the local postman, with his mailbag and postman's cap, made his daily deliveries. He went about his work cheerfully, enjoying his visits with everyone on his mail route. He was more than their mailman; he was a friend to them and he knew their worries without even speaking of it. The lack of snow had brought many changes to Silver Slopes.

He noticed that the bakery wasn't making those delicious scones the visitors loved, with a tall hot cup of coffee or hot chocolate. He noticed the traffic in and out of the gift shop wasn't as bustling as it usually was this time of year. The ski shop had started selling clothing other than the usual winter sportswear.

He was especially friendly with the Doyles--Lucy, Jim and their grandson Mikey. He liked to leave himself some extra time to visit with them if his delivery load allowed. As he walked toward their house with the day's mail, he greeted Jim in the yard cutting fire-wood with Mikey in tow. "Hello Jim. It looks like you have your work for the day with all those tree limbs on the ground. Mikey, are you helping your grandfather today?"

"I am. Grandpa says he can't get anything done without my help. I have to stack all of this wood."

"Well, that's an important job. Make sure you stack them evenly, so they don't fall to the ground. Here, let me help you get that one on the top and then you can start a new pile right next to this one."

"Thanks, Mr. Parsons. I guess I could use some help too."

"That's right. Mr. Parsons brings our mail and helps with wood stacking. Say there, John. What does the post office have for me today?"

"Here's your mail. Not too much today."

"Thank you." Jim set the ax down. "Join me for a cup of coffee?"

"I can use a short break. What about you, Mikey? You coming?"

"No. I have too much work to do," answered Mikey, dili-gently stacking the firewood.

As they made their way toward the house, Mr. Parsons said, "That boy is very special, so polite. And devoted to you and Lucy."

"He is," answered Jim with love and laughter in his eyes. "I need to keep him busy. He keeps us moving that's for sure, but he really does miss his parents, no matter what we do for him."

"It's hard for a young boy, even if it is only for the winter months."

"He keeps hoping for snowfall, but I'm not sure we'll be get-ting any of that. We're at the mercy of Mother Nature and she isn't being kind to us lately."

While Grandpa Jim prepared two cups of coffee, he shared his plan with Mr. Parsons. "Lucy and I are considering getting him a dog. Might make the situation easier for Mikey."

"A dog would be a great companion and playmate too. I can picture him right now outside with a dog at his side."

"Lucy wasn't too happy about the idea at first, but she can't deprive that boy of anything. We're going to surprise him with a trip to the shelter later today. I can't wait to see his excitement when he realizes we can bring one home."

"I guess the next time I come by he will be showing me the newest member of the family. Well, I should be on my way. Give my best to Lucy for me."

Mr. Parsons made his way outside and checked on Mikey's progress before walking toward the next house on his route--Mrs. Downing's. There were several items in his mailbag for her. As friendly and cheerful as Mr. Parsons was with everyone, he was always a little awkward with Mrs. Downing. There wasn't any warmth or friendliness in that woman, never a smile, and never a kind word. "Not everyone can be as welcoming as the Doyles," mumbled Mr. Parsons, as he made his way toward her house. "A strange one she is."

Mrs. Downing noted the postman making his way toward her mailbox and later than his usual time. She was annoyed and needed to let him know it. "Mr. Parsons, I see you are delayed this morning."

"Good morning, Mrs. Downing. I may be a little later than usual, but here I am just the same."

"I don't see it as just the same," she retorted. "Timeliness never goes unnoticed and neither does a lack of it."

"Sorry about that, Mrs. Downing. Well, here is your mail and I wish you a great day."

"Be on your way. No reason to delay any further," said Mrs. Downing as she took her mail and turned back into her house.

"A strange one," mumbled the postman as he made his way to the next house.

Chapter 6

MOTHER NATURE

While the townspeople accepted their snowless season and hoped things would change, the clouds were working on their plan. Fluff prepared himself for his trip to see Mother Nature, as Buff eagerly encouraged him. "Mother Nature will surely understand the problem, and we would all like to know if she would be willing to help. I think she'll be impressed with your request and concern. I'm sure when you tell her of the perfect snowflakes growing in the clouds, she'll be happy to bring about cold weather."

"I don't know what you're talking about, because my vapor is thinning and I may lose all my moisture just thinking about it. You are the one with all the ideas, Buff. Why don't you talk to Mother Nature?"

"I can't talk to Mother Nature. You are our team leader, and the biggest, I might add. She will take you much more seriously than she would ever take me or any of the other clouds. After all, you are the fluffiest one. The softest and puffiest of all!"

"Keep trying to flatter me, but it's not helping one bit," said Fluff trembling.

Just then, Stella, Crystal and Denny presented themselves to Fluff. "We heard you're on your way to speak with Mother Nature for us," said Crystal while checking her perfectly formed six sides. "We are so grateful to you."

"Yes, thanks, Fluff," said Denny enthusiastically. "You're my hero. I know I will be part of the biggest snowman ever made."

"And I want to shimmer on the tip of a sparkling icicle," added Crystal.

"While the two of you have grand plans for yourselves, I just want to be part of a beautiful white blanket," said a frustrated Stella.

"What do mean by grand plans? I just want to stand out and show off my beauty. An icicle is the perfect place for me. After all, an icicle will reflect the light perfectly."

Fluff had no confidence he could get Mother Nature to agree to a snowfall. "You three snowflakes are as beautiful as ever, but I'm not sure this talk with Mother Nature is really going to help our cause. She must have her reasons for keeping you here in the cloud cover and I don't think anything I say will make a difference."

"Now, now Fluff, even with all my fogginess, I can see you're the perfect cloud for this mission," said Foggy.

Drizzle reminded Fluff of what a capable cloud he was. "Yes, I agree. Look how you taught me to use the winds to dry out a little and produce flakes instead of mush. You are a real serious cloud. Mother Nature will see that right away."

"You can make all the difference," added Buff, trying to hide her doubts. "Be on your way now. We can't wait to hear what she says! All of you flakes, stay here with us. This is no trip for fragile snowflakes."

"Yeah, and try to stay still every once in a while. You flakes are wearing me out," said Foggy.

Leaving his friends behind, Fluff, without much hope, made his way upward in the wind toward the Castle of All Seasons, Mother Nature's home. As he did, he practiced his pleadings. He started with "There is no reason to keep the snowflakes in the cloud cover. They need to blanket the earth." Fluff decided that approach sounded a little disrespectful and tried again. "Our snowflakes are much improved, and in fact, quite spectacular this year." No, that is too boastful and besides, Mother Nature might be offended by my taking all the credit for their beauty. "Mother Nature, please set them free. They are causing havoc in the clouds." That sounds a little desperate. Nothing sounds right. He wasn't sure what he was going to say. Maybe he wouldn't even get a chance to see her.

As the wind carried him closer to the castle, he admired the sights and sounds of each of the seasons as he passed: the moisture of the spring rains, the warmth of the summer sun, the brisk autumn breezes and finally, the cold of the winter winds. He thought about his role in the balance of nature as he passed each of the seasons. After all, clouds brought all the moisture the earth needed in any season.

Fluff saw the spring rains bringing green growth to the trees and then the beautiful flowers, the blossoming trees and all those colorful tulips. How beautiful! As he passed summer, he could smell the sweet ripening fruit and the vegetables growing in the gardens under the warm summer sun. In autumn everything was ready to be picked and enjoyed. He saw the pumpkins turning orange and the crisp apples turning red. All four seasons had their special place, but the winter was the most eventful in Fluffs opinion. After all, there wasn't anything more adventurous than a good snowstorm, or even a blizzard, especially for a cloud.

As he traveled, Fluff imagined the whipping winds with snow

falling to the ground in all directions. The trees bending in the wind, with heavy snow-covered branches. Yes, thought Fluff, there was nothing more satisfying for a cloud than to see the earth blanketed by countless beautiful snowflakes and a little sleet mixed in for good measure.

So, lost in his happy thoughts, Fluff was stunned when he was greeted by the cirrostratus clouds guarding the castle. Cirrostratus clouds are the highest-level clouds and Fluff felt dwarfed by them. They looked down on all the other types of clouds. They protected the Castle of All Seasons because they spanned the whole sky in a thin veil of ice particles, forming a wall of ice around the castle.

"What have we here?" asked Cirro, the elder of the cirrostratus guards with a sneer on his face. "What is the reason for your visit?"

"I am here to speak with Mother Nature," answered Fluff, looking up at them with vapor trembling.

"Why would you like an audience with the ever powerful Mother of Nature?"

"Ah, I mean, ah, I mean, it's the town of Silver Slopes, sir," stuttered Fluff. "They haven't had a snowfall in a very long time. We have some beautiful flakes this year and we, I mean, I, was wondering if we can release them soon."

"I think Mother Nature knows better than you when, and if, a snowfall is possible. Don't you?"

"I know, I know she does. But I wonder if I can speak with her about it."

"I don't think we want to bother Mother Nature with your wondering, do you? After all she is very busy controlling the weather and all the earth with just the right balance. She has no time to be concerned with your beautiful flakes and small little town. Off with you!"

Saddened but relieved, Fluff started to deflate. "Well, I tried my best," he mumbled to himself as he turned to leave. "I didn't think this would work anyway."

Just as he was about to float away from the castle gate, Mother Nature appeared. "Cirro, let me hear of this cumulous cloud's concerns. Let him in."

Peering beyond the castle gate, Fluff saw Mother Nature in a gown of flowing green leaves and a crown of spring flowers. Her hair was as golden as the summer sun and her eyes as blue as the sky. In her hand was a scepter of sparkling jewels that glistened as she moved it. She was beautiful and a little scary, but she had a kind face with a reassuring smile.

Behind her was the magnificent Castle of All Seasons, and Fluff was in awe of its beauty. It had four towers, so tall, they seemed to reach for the stars, each one representing one of the seasons. The first tower was the spring tower. It was wrapped in flowers, with birds of every color building their nests. The summer tower sparkled in the sun, decorated with vegetable vines and flowering fruit trees. The winter tower was covered in sparkling icicles, with frozen red holly berries and crystalized, blue spruce branches circling it as far as the eye could see. The last one reflected every color of the autumn season. It was red, purple, orange and yellow. Each tower was more beautiful than the last.

Fluff felt so dwarfed by the beauty of Mother Nature and her castle that he was even more convinced this trip was a bad idea. "I shouldn't be here," he said. "After all, I am only a lowly cloud. I'll just be on my way."

"Nonsense!" answered Cirro. "You have requested an audience and now you will state your case. Mother Nature is awaiting you!"

"If you insist," answered Fluff, a shiver running through him.

He made his way beyond the castle gate and addressed Mother Nature with respect. "Your Majesty, Majestic Mother of all Things Nature, Queen of the Cloud Cover…"

"That's enough. There is no reason to fear me. Just tell me why you have traveled outside of your cloud zone to speak with me."

"About that," stuttered Fluff. "I can get back there very quickly, no problem."

Mother Nature interrupted Fluff once again and encouraged him to get to the point. "I'm listening," she said kindly.

"Well, you see, I am from the area over the village of Silver Slopes, and we clouds were wondering if you had a plan for some snowfall this year. We have some very restless, I mean, very beautiful, snowflakes this year and we would like to release them soon. We were hoping that could happen soon. Or soonish at least."

"I see," answered Mother Nature. "I understand your concern, but there is a problem in Silver Slopes, and I have not been able to release the snowflakes in recent years. You see, not everyone in Silver Slopes welcomes our handiwork. There is one person in the town that is very against our beautiful snowflakes. It seems her heart has hardened to the beauty of winter."

"One person in town that isn't very nice means there has to be another winter without snow?"

Mother Nature patiently explained the problem in Silver Slopes. "Years ago, Mrs. Downing had an unfortunate mishap in the snow. She took a sled ride she will never forget, and her burning anger and embarrassment over it has created a thick blanket of angry hot air between the clouds and the village of Silver Slopes. Every time she thinks of snow, her embarrassment feeds that blanket with more hot air. Even the redness of her cheeks warms the atmosphere. I am afraid that blanket is so thick, it has become permanent. No snowflake could survive the journey through it without turning to water."

"What do I tell the other clouds and those fidgety flakes? There must be something you can do!"

"I can't help you, Fluff. Tell them it is up to the townspeople of Silver Slopes to warm the heart of their neighbor, Mrs. Downing. As her heart overflows with love, she will heal from her shame and that blanket of hot air will turn cold enough for a snowfall. We can do nothing," said Mother Nature. "Now return to the others and take your post."

"Yes, Majestic Mother of all things nature, great Queen..."

"That's enough, Fluff. Just get going."

"Okay, Mother. Thank you for seeing me," said Fluff as he turned away and made his way outside the castle gate. He trekked back to Silver Slopes, deflating his vapor all the way. Even the passing seasons couldn't lift his spirits.

Buff, nervous and excited, looked for any sign of Fluff returning. "I see him," she said. "But I'm afraid he looks much smaller than when he left. I wonder why?"

"What do you mean smaller?" asked Stella. "He shouldn't be smaller. What has happened to him?"

"I'm not sure. Maybe it's my eyes. They are a little misty sometimes."

"What do you see, Hazel?" asked Drizzle. Foggy and I can't see him clearly.

"I think I see a shrunken Fluff coming our way."

"Oh, this can't be a good sign," cried Crystal.

"He probably just wore himself out on his way," said Denny confidently.

Buff nervously met Fluff and helped him get back to his post. "Oh Fluff, what has happened to you? Did you have to go through a storm on your way? I know how those storms can be. Was it a hurricane or a blizzard?"

"The news isn't good," said Fluff, panting and wheezing. "No, I didn't have to go through any storms, but Mother Nature said there is nothing she can do to help us. There is someone in Silver Slopes causing a cover of hot air over the village. No snowflake would survive the journey through it! Every time this villager thinks of snow, her anger and shame puts more hot air into the sky. At least, that's how I understand it. There isn't anything Mother Nature can do. She said this blanket of hot air is permanent!"

Denny, Crystal and Stella cried in unison, "OH NO! No Snow!"

"All this beauty will go to waste," wailed Crystal. "It's all over for us, forever."

"I, for one, don't think we should just give up," said Hazel adamantly. "We didn't give up on flake-making and that turned out amazingly."

Fluff had a defeated tone. "She said there is nothing we can do, and we don't even know anything about this Mrs. Downing. She just can't get over some sled ride gone wrong."

"Mrs. Downing? Let me think. Now where have I heard that name?" wondered Foggy.

Buff suddenly realized that she knew of Mrs. Downing. "I remember that sled ride! It ended in a collision with a holly bush. Berries and twigs were everywhere. I guess she never got over it. I'll show you where she is." Buff pointed out Mrs. Downing's house to everyone. "She's hardly ever outside."

"She may never be outside, but boy is she causing a problem for us," said a defeated Foggy.

Chapter 7

BUSTER

Totally unaware of the dire circumstances discussed in the clouds, Mikey was happily playing with his new puppy. It was a handsome white puppy with brown floppy ears and one brown spot on his back. His tail wagged back and forth, as Mikey tried to train the active puppy.

"Now Buster, if you want a treat you have to give me the stick back. Drop it, Buster!" Buster wanted to play tug of war with the stick and barked in response to Mikey prying it away from him. "Now, Buster, go fetch," said Mikey as he threw the stick as far across the yard as he could. Instead of chasing the stick, Buster jumped up toward the treat bag.

Jim and Lucy watched from the kitchen window, enjoying the interaction between their grandson and his new puppy. "Just look at how happy Mikey is with that little dog," said Lucy. "He's really good with him too."

"I knew it was just the right time. He needs a playmate and a puppy is perfect."

"You were right. It makes me happy just watching him. Look at that puppy run. It's a good thing we have fencing in the front yard. We have to make sure we don't lose that dog."

"Who is that coming up the front walkway?" asked Jim.

"Why, it's Mrs. Downing. What could she possibly want?"

"I can't imagine it can be anything good," answered Jim. "We hardly ever see that woman outside of her house. Look, she stopped to talk to Mikey. I'd better get out there fast."

"You go ahead. I'll grab my jacket and meet you out there."

Grandpa Jim made his way to the front door. As he stepped outside, he saw Mikey and Mrs. Downing in conversation as Buster joyfully jumped up and down to greet their neighbor. Mrs. Downing was speaking with Mikey, pointing a stern finger at him with an expression of displeasure on her round, angry face.

"You see what I mean? That dog is a brute! You need to make sure that dog does not frighten or hurt my Bianca. She is a very special cat, and I can't have your dog terrorizing her or worse," said Mrs. Downing, all the while shooing Buster away. "Down, you bad dog!"

"Hello neighbor. Is there a problem here?" asked Jim.

"Grandpa, she says Buster is going to hurt her cat. I told her no. That's not right. He would never hurt her cat."

"This is Mrs. Downing. Please be polite."

"But Grandpa, I tried to tell her Buster is good. And he probably would like her cat."

"Take Buster inside and I will speak with Mrs. Downing."

"Okay. I'll go inside but I know Buster is a good dog. Bye, Mrs. Downing," said Mikey as he guided his new puppy into the house.

As Lucy made her way toward her husband and neighbor, she passed Mikey and could see the tears rolling down his face. "Mikey, why are you crying?"

"She thinks Buster is a bad dog and he is going to hurt her cat," Mikey answered with his voice trembling.

"She does?" asked Lucy, giving Mikey a comforting hug. "Well, why does she think that? He's a good dog and so cute too."

Mikey looked up at his grandmother and asked, "We can keep him, can't we?"

"Of course, we can. He's your dog. Grandpa and I will take care of this. You go ahead inside and give Buster some water. He's been working hard at fetching that stick."

Annoyed, Lucy approached Mrs. Downing in serious conversation with her husband. "Hello Mrs. Downing. Is there a problem?"

"No problem yet, but I had to remind your grandson that there is a very special member of my family that I need to protect--my cat, Bianca."

"Is Bianca in danger, Mrs. Downing?" asked Lucy innocently.

Jim, on the other hand, was ready to address the problem head on. "Let's not overreact. There is no reason to fear that new puppy. Our yard is fenced, and Mikey keeps a close eye on him. In fact, if Bianca is the white cat I see making her way through our yard, I think you should keep a closer eye on her."

"Well, it isn't my cat you are seeing in your yard. My Bianca always keeps close by. She likes to spend her time stretching in the sunshine right by my front door. She never ventures away. I just want to be sure she'll be safe in her own yard." Mrs. Downing sniffed, as if Jim didn't smell very good. "I am just making everyone aware of my expectations. We all just need to keep to ourselves and there shouldn't be a problem. That's all I needed to say, so I'll be on my way. Have a good day." Mrs. Downing turned and returned the way she came.

Jim shook his head as he watched her leave. "Do you believe that woman? Anyone that needs to interact with her is left in disbelief. 'Have a good day,' she says. Bullying a young boy over a little puppy. Unbelievable!"

"Hush, Jim. We need to get inside and check on Mikey. He is so upset. Poor thing. He went into the house with tears rolling down his face."

Chapter 8
MESSAGE IN THE CLOUDS

*U*p in the cloud cover, Fluff and Buff, along with those restless snowflakes were more discouraged than ever. Mrs. Downing's visit with the Doyles made them realize what a hopeless situation they had on their hands. Her heart was not warming at all. In fact, she was being heartless with that poor boy and his cute little dog. All they could do was look down upon the village and sulk.

Fluff voiced what was on the mind of each one of them. "I don't see how this situation will get any better. I'm afraid we have another year without a snowfall. We may never see snow in Silver Slopes."

Denny, forever the optimist, was the only one with a hopeful outlook. "Well, she does love her cat. That's something. Isn't it?"

The others, altogether said, "Oh Denny!"

"There must be something we can do. I think we need to get creative about this situation," said a determined Hazel. "I know I'm being clear sighted about this, despite all of my haze. We can't just give up!"

"We're only clouds. All I can do is rain over her house. Yes, maybe that's an idea. I always have some rain I can do without.

That might get her attention," offered Drizzle.

"Yeah, and I can get down as low as possible and surround her house in some of my fog. She will have to notice us then," said Foggy. "My fog can be very dense."

"I think we're forgetting we need to warm her heart, not overwhelm her with rain and fog. I think I have a better idea," said Buff.

All the clouds gathered together to take direction from Buff. It was decided to send Mrs. Downing a message the only way they could. They argued and bickered over who would be first and who'd be next, but they finally lined up across the sky.

"I'm not sure I can manage this very well," said a doubtful Foggy.

"All you have to do is form a '*T*' and an '*O*', Foggy," Hazel said. "You have the easiest word. I have to manage four letters, *L*, *O*, *V* and an *E*. Now that is hard." She stuck out her tongue, concentrating, as she practiced re-shaping herself as best she could.

"This is a crazy idea. How do you spell *Downing*?" asked Fluff. "You know I am not good under pressure. Why do I have the hardest word?"

"You have the longest word because you are the biggest cloud," said Buff. "I don't know how to spell it either, but just do the best you can."

"Should I put a period after the '*R*'?" asked a confused Drizzle. "Maybe I can use a raindrop for the period."

"How can you use a raindrop for the period? Just forget the period. Concentrate on the rest of it," instructed Buff. "Get ready, because as soon as we see her walk out of her house, it is show time!"

"What do all of us snowflakes do? How can we help?" asked Stella.

"Yes, we can help too," offered Denny.

"You flakes just hang onto each other so you don't get released as raindrops!" answered Buff.

"There is that raindrop word again! It's so upsetting," said Crystal. "I don't know what happens to me when I hear that word."

Mrs. Downing prepared to make her weekly trip into town. She needed food for Bianca and would probably buy her a new toy too. She'd noticed Bianca had gained a little weight. It wasn't good for her health. A new toy may encourage her to get a little more exercise. One of those toy mice, dangling from a string would be more than Bianca could resist.

The clouds saw the front door to Mrs. Downing's house opening and immediately took their places in the sky. Buff tried to take the lead and started to compress herself into an O, followed by a U and then an R. The other clouds followed and started to roll around and curve themselves as best they could.

"What is happening here!" exclaimed Denny. "I like to twirl about, but this is even too much for me."

Crystal was horrified by the possibility of part of her shape being damaged in the process. "I know we want to be part of a snowfall, but this is not what I had in mind. My sides are being crushed in ways I could never imagine."

Stella added, "This time I have to agree with you, Crystal. This is not the best environment for growing flakes!"

Buff called out to the clouds and the snowflakes. "Hang in there, everyone. Hazel, you have a very important word. Try harder with the L and the O; otherwise she won't get the message at all."

Panting, Hazel responded, "I can just about manage the V and the E. IF I do the L and the O, I will lose the V and the E."

"Just one more letter and I will be done. Just an S, that's all I need," panted Drizzle. "Forget the period, that's for sure."

Fluff grunted, "I have three letters, but who knows how many more I need. I just can't manage any more."

With more effort than they realized would be necessary, and with chaos abounding, they took the shape of the message for Mrs. Downing. Strung across the sky were the words, OUR LOVE TO MRS DOWNING, but it actually looked like "O…R ..VE..O MR..D….NG", and barely that at best.

"What a strange cloud formation!" exclaimed Mrs. Downing. "Well, at least they aren't gray clouds, just white and puffy. No snow anytime soon." And she got into her car, proceeding to go about her errands.

The clouds exhaled and regained their pre-message shape as the snowflakes examined each other for any serious damage.

"Well, that was a failed experiment. Any other brilliant ideas, anyone?" said Hazel sarcastically.

"Be nice, Hazel," responded Drizzle. "You didn't do such a great job yourself. All you managed was the *VE*."

"At least we tried," added Buff.

"Yes, we tried, and then we failed. It's hopeless!" said Fluff, letting out a last large puff of vapor as he took his usual puffy shape.

"As I said before, she does love that cat," added Denny, reminding everyone of his previous thought.

Everyone shouted out in unison, "Oh, Denny!"

"Well, she does," answered Denny defensively.

Chapter 9

AROUND TOWN

*M*r. Parsons was making his rounds with the mail when he decided to stop at the pet store to buy a toy for Mikey's new dog.

As he reached the pet shop, he was greeted by Captain Finnerty of the town police department, a portly man with a round face. "Hello John, good to see you this morning."

"Hello, Captain, keeping law and order in our beautiful town I see."

"Yes, but mostly I'm enjoying this brisk weather and sunshine. How is your day going?"

"I am about to buy a dog toy. John and Lucy adopted a dog for Mikey Doyle from the shelter. I'm sure that boy is overjoyed. I thought I'd stop in and meet his new friend."

"A new puppy for Mikey! Maybe I'll take a walk with you. I'd like to meet their new addition too and some exercise will do me good. Do you mind if I come along?"

"I'll meet up with you as soon as I pick up a dog toy at Martha's pet shop. I'll be right out."

"Take your time," said the captain as he patted his rather large belly. I want to take a look in the bakery window to see if they still have those cinnamon buns I can't resist. I'll meet you on the corner."

Mr. Parsons made his way toward the pet shop and noticed Mrs. Downing inside before opening the shop door. He hesitated and braced himself for what was sure to be an uncomfortable meeting. Once he was inside Martha, the shop owner, greeted Mr. Parsons with her usual friendly smile. "Hello John. I guess you have some mail for me today?"

"Yes. In fact, I do have mail for you." He handed the mail to Martha, then turned to Mrs. Downing. "I think I have a few things for you as well, Mrs. Downing. Would you like to take them now? Otherwise, I can leave them in your mailbox."

"I'd prefer my mailbox where it belongs."

"No problem. Your mailbox it is. I just dropped by to get a toy for Mikey Doyle's new dog. Is there something you can recommend, Martha?"

"Yes, Mrs. Downing was just telling me about Mikey's new dog."

Mrs. Downing didn't waste any time sharing her opinion of the new dog. "I'm afraid that dog is a danger to my Bianca. I had to make sure the Doyles understood my concerns, so I went right over there to speak with them about keeping that dog out of my yard. Cats and dogs aren't the best of friends, you know."

"I am sure it will be fine," Martha said calmly. "Actually, I think it's better to introduce the two. Dogs and cats can be respectful of one another, even in the same house."

"Well, Bianca and that dog don't live in the same house. I made it clear to the Doyles how we needed to handle the situation."

Mr. Parsons sighed at the thought of Mrs. Downing's talk with the Doyles. He hoped Mikey was spared that conversation. "I am sure you made yourself clear to the Doyles. I, for one, think a new dog is just what that boy needs. So, Martha, let's pick out that dog toy."

"Sure, let's take a look at the squeaky dog toys. Dogs love the sound they make."

Frustrated, Mrs. Downing left. She didn't know why no one understood her fears. Bianca was all she had, and she needed to protect her.

As Mr. Parsons and Martha looked through the dog toys, he took a moment to share his feelings. "I don't see how Mrs. Downing can think a new puppy for a little boy is a problem. After all, she treasures her pet too."

Martha, a kind-hearted soul, knew Mrs. Downing from her weekly visits caring for her cat. "I know, John, but I do feel for Mrs. Downing. She is a lonely woman you know and I don't think she has been the same since that terrible sled accident."

"I had forgotten about that accident. It was awful, but she wasn't hurt. I remember she was very embarrassed and angry, but that is no reason to be so cold-hearted. I just hope she had some kindness in her when she spoke to the Doyles about the new puppy."

Looking over the dog toys, Mr. Parsons chose a long caterpillar. "I'll take this one so Mikey can play tug of war with his new dog."

"Good choice. I'm sure Mikey and his dog will love it."

Chapter 10

BIANCA MISSING

*C*aptain Finnerty joined Mr. Parsons on his mail delivery route and the two made their way to the Doyle's home on the edge of town. After the earlier visit with Mrs. Downing, the Doyles welcomed these friendly visitors. Mikey was overjoyed with the new dog toy and happy to show his dog's delight in rough and tumble play. Buster loved pulling on the caterpillar with all of his strength, shaking his head from side to side, and growling.

While the Doyles and their guests enjoyed their visit, things were not going well with their neighbor Mrs. Downing. She had prepared Bianca's dinner, but Bianca was nowhere to be found. She searched high and low, under beds and atop bookcases, as cats have many hiding places. She checked underneath and behind the sofa as well as in between the cushions. She looked on the windowsills of all the feline's favorite windows. But no Bianca.

After exhausting Bianca's usual spots inside the house, she remembered letting Bianca out earlier, but didn't remember letting her in since. "She must be waiting outside the door for me to let her in, poor baby," she murmured. Confidently, Mrs. Downing opened the door wide, expecting to see her waiting patiently and was surprised to see that Bianca was not there. Now Mrs. Downing was so panicked, she couldn't remember if she last saw her cat inside or outside. "Bianca, where are you? I have your dinner for you," she called out, expecting her cat to come out from behind the bushes or down from a tree. "It isn't like Bianca to miss a meal. What could have happened to her?" Mrs. Downing's distress turned to anger as she glanced out toward her neighbor's yard. This could only mean one thing. That dog had been up to no good. "This is exactly what I feared would happen!" she growled, and decided to pay the Doyles a visit.

Buff alerted Fluff of the newest developments in Silver Slopes. "Oh Fluff, we have a problem. Mrs. Downing has lost her cat. She was calling her from the front door and the cat is nowhere to be found."

"Buff, we have a hopeless situation and you're concerned about Mrs. Downing's missing cat? Cats always love to hide and play games. Now, these snowflakes bouncing about, *that* is a problem." Fluff was distracted, trying to contain the active snowflakes racing to-and-fro within the clouds. Stella, Denny and Crystal, along with countless other snowflakes, were scampering in a circle, playing tag. They were doing what snowflakes will do--dancing throughout the clouds, catching particles and water droplets, crystalizing larger and larger. Watching them, Fluff added dizzily, "The real problem is releasing these flakes. I don't think I can hold them any longer. I'm thinking we need to make a snowball out of them and send them to the ground."

Ignoring Fluff, Buff continued to watch the activity in Silver Slopes, and specifically, the activity at Mrs. Downing's house. The cat wasn't visible anywhere and Buff began to panic along with Mrs. Downing. If that cat was lost, there wasn't any hope of warming Mrs. Downing's heart to a winter wonderland. "I'm not sure where that cat has gone," said Buff, "and Mrs. Downing is making her way to the house next door. Oh no. She looks angry!"

Fluff asked, "And tell me how this is more important than containing these snowflakes?"

"Mrs. Downing's cat? The white, fluffy cat with the bushy tail?" asked Foggy.

"Yes, Foggy. The white cat!" replied a frustrated Buff.

"Never mind. I was just asking," said Foggy.

Chapter 11

BUSTER ACCUSED

Mrs. Downing rang the doorbell at the Doyle's house, interrupting the joy and laughter of everyone playing tug of war with the active Buster. A surprised Lucy invited Mrs. Downing inside.

Mrs. Downing ignored the invitation. "Is my Bianca here? She hasn't come home and I'm afraid my fears have come true. Has that dog chased her, or worse, hurt her?"

"Bianca? No, we haven't seen your cat. Please come in. We have Captain Finnerty here. Perhaps you can ask him." Grandma Lucy nervously led Mrs. Downing into the living room to the surprise of Grandpa Jim and his company. Lucy explained the visit to the others. "It seems Mrs. Downing's cat is missing and she thought we may have seen her."

All at once, the joy drained from the faces of Jim, Mikey, Captain Finnerty, and Mr. Parsons. Only Buster was oblivious to the change in everyone's mood and continued to play with his new toy. Mikey tried taking the caterpillar away from him and only made the situation worse. After all, Buster only knew to continue to pull at the toy.

Mrs. Downing surveyed the room and seemed even more

convinced that her Bianca had a run in with Buster and was either hurt or refused to come home to such a dangerous situation. There was no possibility that such a happy-go-lucky dog would bother chasing a cat, but everyone knew, until that cat was found, there would be no convincing Mrs. Downing.

"My Bianca never wanders far from my house. I can only think that new dog of yours has somehow caused her to run and hide," Mrs. Downing droned on. "I tried warning you this would be a problem and everyone thought I was acting foolishly. Now my precious Bianca is nowhere to be found."

Lucy felt compassion and tried to encourage her. "Mrs. Downing, cats often wander, but they always find their way home. There is no need to worry."

Captain Finnerty, being an authority figure in the community, stepped in to take charge of this situation. "I can put our best detectives on this case. We are sure to find her because, after all, we are the experts. As an expert I can say there is no reason to suspect this friendly animal. He is just a harmless puppy."

Mr. Parsons, as an objective participant, believed he could help calm Mrs. Downing's fears as well. "I would be happy to help look for her while on my mail route. I can talk to everyone and find out if there have been any sightings of the cat."

Now Mikey, with eyes tearing and voice trembling as well, was also distressed over the missing Bianca, but defended his dog nonetheless. "Just because Buster is a dog, doesn't mean he would hurt your cat. You aren't being fair. Buster could probably find her for you."

"There is no need for help from that dog!"

"I have had just about enough discussion about this innocent puppy," said Grandpa. "If you need help locating your cat, I am willing to look for her, but you must stop upsetting my grandson. Let's be logical about this and take a look around. Mikey, you stay inside with your grandmother. Captain Finnerty, Mr. Parsons and I will look around. It's starting to get dark, so let's get to it."

Lucy offered to make Mrs. Downing a cup of tea while the men prepared themselves for their search. Jim searched the cupboard for some kind of treat to lure Bianca from her hiding place. He settled on a can of tuna fish and proceeded to open it. Postman John pulled a flashlight from his mailbag so he could have a better look behind bushes and up into the trees as he delivered the mail. Captain Finnerty made a call to the police station to put the other police officers on the lookout for a long-haired white cat, just in case she'd wandered farther than they expected.

While everyone moved into action, Mikey cuddled with his dog on the sofa for comfort. "Oh Buster, you haven't seen Bianca, have you?" Buster looked up at Mikey with the most innocent of eyes, then rested his head on Mikey's arm for a much-needed nap.

The men, all geared up for their search, walked outside and began discussing their search strategy, with Captain Finnerty in charge. Mr. Parsons was to continue his mail delivery, ringing each doorbell to alert the community to the missing Bianca. Jim was to thoroughly search his property, as well as Mrs. Downing's, in case Bianca had not ventured very far. Captain Finnerty would go back to the police station to command a search party to comb town shops and parks. "Remember to report to me if there are any signs of that cat, or if anyone has any information about it. As your captain, I will be in charge of this operation and we will find Bianca safe and sound; I am sure of it." With that, the captain left the other two to their missions and proceeded to the police station while calling for Bianca with each step, "Here kitty, kitty. Bianca. Come out, come out wherever you are. We have some special treats for you!"

As Mr. Parsons rang each doorbell on his mail delivery route, concern was growing in the community.

"No, I haven't seen Bianca at all today," said one villager.

"She doesn't usually come into my yard," said another.

"Bianca? I don't think I know what she looks like," remarked most of the villagers.

Even though there wasn't any information on Bianca's whereabouts, everyone questioned was willing to search their yards and report any findings. After all, the people of Silver Slopes believed the worries of one were the worries of all.

Chapter 12

MOTHER NATURE ARRIVES

uff kept a keen eye on the activity in Silver Slopes, hoping to see some change in the warm air blanketing the town. Fluff's attention was on the ever-active snow flurries growing heavier with each passing moment.

While most of the snowflakes were all fun and games, Stella was just as concerned as Buff. "Buff, do you see any progress down there? I think it may be getting a little colder. I feel it."

"I thought so too, Stella, I think there may be a cold mist coming our way. I wonder what this cold mist is about because I don't see anything happening in Silver Slopes to give us any hope. The only thing I see is a lot of activity surrounding Mrs. Downing and her cat, and I think she's less happy than ever. It's hard to tell from up here."

Buff peered in every direction, until she caught sight of the cirrostratus clouds coming their way. "I think I know what's happening, Stella. We're going to have a visit from Mother Nature herself. She's coming this way. Quick, alert the snowflakes! We have to be on our best behavior."

Buff alerted all the local cloud cover to prepare for the arrival of Mother Nature as Stella tried to get all the other snowflakes to pay attention.

Cirro, leading the way for Mother Nature's arrival, was aghast at the chaos of clouds and snowflakes. "What have we here!" he exclaimed. "Mother Nature is to arrive, and she will not be happy with the state of the sky over Silver Slopes. Stand at attention everyone and stop that racket."

With that, Denny stopped short of crashing into Cirro, which would have nearly ruined his beautiful shape. "Who are you?" asked Denny.

"I am the commanding cirrostratus guard of the Castle of All Seasons and Mother Nature depends on me for her protection," answered Cirro.

"But what are you protecting her from?" Denny said innocently. "I thought she was the mother of everything."

Denny's challenging question led to Cirro's confusion. "Oh. Well, I am not sure what from, but she depends on me, or maybe I depend on her? It's all so confusing." He remembered his mission and re-asserted himself. "In any case, I command all of you to attention."

Clouds and snowflakes alike paused and were awed by the stately presence and the beauty of their mother making her way toward them. Mother Nature glanced around and quickly understood the problems Fluff had told her about. "I've come to see for myself the difficulties over the village of Silver Slopes. I can see what you mean, Fluff. There are some beautiful snowflakes here and things are getting quite heavy for the cloud cover."

Crystal beamed with pride at the notice of her beauty. "I knew she would help us if she just saw how perfectly I glisten," she whispered to Stella.

Finding it difficult to stay still, Denny needed some information. "How long is this going to take, Stella? I don't know if I can stand at attention for very long."

Stella hushed both Crystal and Denny, ignoring them both, so she could listen to the discussion between Mother Nature and the clouds.

"Yes, your highness, Mother," answered Fluff. "It hasn't been easy for any of us."

Buff made her way toward Mother Nature to present her plea. "Something is happening in Silver Slopes, but I'm not sure what it could be. It seems Mrs. Downing has lost her cat and she isn't very happy about it. I'm afraid this is making our situation worse than before."

"Yes, I know of the situation with Mrs. Downing's cat. The birds have alerted me and in fact, I believe this may be the answer to your problem. I think we may have found a way to heal Mrs. Downing of her hardened heart. Do not lose hope just yet."

Curious as always, Buff tried to get more information from Mother Nature. She asked, "How does her missing cat help us? She seems to be angrier than before. Please tell us."

"Trust me, Buff. I think Mrs. Downing's heart will overflow with love when she finds her missing cat. If not, these beautiful snow flurries can travel down in a rainfall. I know that might be disappointing, but the earth needs rain as well you know. Let's stay hopeful."

As Mother Nature and her attendants departed, the snow-flakes over Silver Slopes burst into tears.

"What is all this crying over a missing cat?" asked Foggy. "I know where that cat is. You know my mistiness is sometimes very low to the ground so I can see a lot more of what goes on."

"Sure, you do, Foggy. You haven't had a clear thought in years," said Hazel.

"I do know where that cat is. She's in the barn next door. I saw her walking in there yesterday. I don't think she's come out since," said Foggy confidently.

Buff was excited. "She's in the barn? That's great news!"

"What are we going to do with that bit of information? It's just another bit of information we can't spell out," said a defeated Fluff.

"I could rain just over the barn. That might get someone's attention," offered Drizzle.

"Again with the rain, Drizzle?" asked Buff.

"Well, I don't think I have it in me to try and form anymore letters. Anyway, we weren't very good at it last time." Fluff considered their options and settled on the easiest solution he could think of. "All we can do is settle around that barn. It might give them the idea to look in there."

Chapter 13

THE BARN

*L*ate into the night, the search party continued to look for Bianca. Even though the neighborhood, and in fact, the whole village had been alerted, no one had any information about where she may have gone. They tried their best, looking behind bushes, up in the trees and anywhere they could think of, to find her. Mrs. Downing left the Doyle's house discouraged and upset, walking back to her house in tears. The poor woman was beside herself at the loss of her beautiful cat.

The next morning, Lucy packed up a batch of her homemade muffins to bring next door. She could never see someone suffering without trying to help. She worried for her neighbor and used the muffins as a way to check on her.

"Jim, I'm going over to Mrs. Downing to drop off these muffins. The poor woman may need some company. Mikey is outside with Buster still trying to teach that dog to play fetch, so keep an eye on him. And keep him away from the barn. I'm not sure why, but it looks especially gloomy over in that direction this morning."

Reading the paper at the kitchen table, Jim didn't even try to discourage Lucy this time. He also felt sorry for Mrs. Downing and the loss of her cat.

While passing through the front yard, Lucy smiled as she heard Mikey giving Buster instructions. "Buster, you have to bring me the stick after I throw it. Then I'll give you a treat. Are you ready? Now fetch!" Buster jumped in the air, trying to intercept the stick, but confusedly stared at the treat bag after he missed the stick in mid-air. "Buster, go get it," said Mikey, a little frustrated, as Buster lunged for the treat bag.

Jim chuckled at the scene he was witnessing from the kitchen window, watching his grandson trying to train the willful puppy. The boy needed some guidance getting the puppy to play by the rules, so he joined Mikey outside. "Don't throw that stick very far. I think you need to throw it down right in front of you. As soon as he picks up that stick, give him a treat. That should help him understand."

Mikey, grateful for some help, did as his grandfather instructed. Mikey threw the stick right in front of him and amazingly, Buster picked it up in his teeth. "Good boy. Now you can have a treat." Buster was grateful for a dog biscuit and made his way to a quiet place to enjoy it. "He did it Grandpa, finally!"

"I see that. Good job."

Thoughtful and compassionate, Mikey thought of poor Mrs. Downing and her missing cat. He knew how sad he would be if he couldn't find Buster. "You didn't find Mrs. Downing's cat, did you Grandpa?"

"No, we didn't, but she may still turn up somewhere. We have everyone in town looking out for her. She will probably make her way back home any minute now."

"I hope so," answered Mikey. "Mrs. Downing will be so much happier when Bianca comes back home."

"That's right. Her cat is her family, and she wants her home safe and sound." Trying to turn Mikey's attention away from worry about Bianca, Grandpa Jim picked up the stick and added,

"Why don't you keep training this dog to fetch. I think he's finished his treat already."

Mikey took the stick and threw it just a little farther this time. Buster knew just what to do, fetch it and bring it back to Mikey. "Good job, Buster. Now you get another treat."

"You are doing a fine job with that dog, Mikey. I'll be watching you from the window inside. And stay away from the barn. It's a little foggy over that way."

As Mikey continued to play fetch with his puppy, Buster seemed less and less interested in the biscuits. Instead of eating his treat, he took off into the barn, ignoring Mikey's call. Just as quickly, he ran back to Mikey with tail wagging, waiting for him to throw the stick again.

Remembering his grandfather's instructions, he reprimanded Buster for going into the barn. "Where do you think you're going, Buster? You don't need to go into the barn to eat your treat. Silly dog!" Each time, Buster took the treat from Mikey and ran into the barn with it. This time, ignoring his grandfather's warning, Mikey ran after him. What could Buster be doing in there with his treat?

Watching from the kitchen window, Jim, curious and concerned, decided to follow both of them. Making his way to the barn, he could only imagine that Buster had found a safe place to bury his dog biscuits. After all, Buster had eaten quite a few of them already, and may have decided to put them in a safe place for later.

As he walked into the barn, he saw Mikey kneeling down in the far corner, with Buster sitting next to him. Unable to see what Mikey and Buster were doing, he walked towards them as he called out, "Mikey, is everything okay back there?"

"Grandpa, come and see what Buster found. You won't believe it!"

When Jim peered over Mikey's shoulders, he saw Bianca nestled in the hay. It appeared she was a new mother. There were three adorable kittens, and the proud Bianca was feeding her family. Amazingly, it seemed Buster knew where she was all along. All around Bianca and her babies were the uneaten dog treats that Buster had brought to them. Instead of hurting Bianca, he was trying to care for her and her kittens.

"Aren't they cute, Grandpa, and so tiny!"

"Well, look at that. They really are, and I think Buster thinks so too. They are so well-tucked in the corner. I didn't see them when I checked the barn last night."

"Mrs. Downing will be so happy. Now instead of one cat, she'll have a whole family. Quick, let's go and tell her we found Bianca!"

Mikey and his grandfather quickly walked toward Mrs. Downing's house with Buster following close behind. Out of breath, they rang her doorbell with more excitement than they could contain. Mrs. Downing answered the door with Lucy standing behind her. Mikey was so excited, as soon as the door opened, he blurted out, "Mrs. Downing, we found Bianca and she has a new family!"

"You found her? Where is she? Is she hurt?" she asked fretfully.

Jim tried to fill in the blanks over Mikey's excitement and Mrs. Downing's fears. "Bianca is just fine. We found her in our barn, and it seems she is a new mother. She has three adorable kittens she is caring for."

Mrs. Downing, overwhelmed with joy and relief, exclaimed, "My Bianca is a new mother! I can't believe you found her. Please, lead me to her. I can't wait to see them."

Mrs. Downing, Jim and Lucy walked into the barn, with Mikey leading the way and Buster trailing behind. Mrs. Downing was so happy, she was crying tears of joy. "Oh Bianca, I've missed you so much–and look at your beautiful kittens." She picked up each kitten, one at a time, and caressed them against her cheek. Two of them were white with black markings and one was all white, just like Bianca.

As Mrs. Downing admired Bianca's family, her cold heart melted in love and thankfulness for her neighbors. She couldn't deny that the villagers did all they could to find her precious cat. "They are just as beautiful as my Bianca. I can't thank you enough for finding them."

Jim explained to Mrs. Downing the events leading up to the discovery of Bianca and her kittens. "Actually, you can thank Buster. If you notice, he was offering his dog treats to Bianca. Mikey found her because he followed Buster into the barn."

"What a clever dog you have, Mikey, and very generous too. I am so sorry I ever accused him of hurting Bianca. He's a good dog, just like you said, Mikey. He found my precious Bianca for me."

Lucy was also crying tears of joy for such a happy ending. "I'm so happy for you, Mrs. Downing. These kittens are a wonderful addition to your home. I think we should get this new family settled inside. It feels like it's getting a little colder out here."

With that, the four of them carried Bianca and her three kittens into Mrs. Downing's home, with, the hero Buster, leading the way, of course. They prepared a cozy spot for the new family, in the corner of the living room and everyone breathed a sigh of relief, even Buster, as he settled down next to them.

Chapter 14

CALLING ALL SNOWFLAKES

*W*anting the attention of the cloud cover over the village of Silver Slopes, Mother Nature instructed Cirro to sound the snowfall call on his trumpet. Recognizing the call to order, all of the clouds came to attention, waiting for the important announcement. With complete quiet, Mother Nature proceeded. "I am happy to announce that we are ready for a magnificent snowfall over the town of Silver Slopes!"

All of the surrounding clouds, both high and low, started cheering, and all of the sparkling snowflakes started to twirl with joy and excitement. The clouds would soon be relieved of the overactive snowflakes and the snowflakes could float to the ground in a magical snowfall dance. Everyone's dream of a beautiful snowfall would finally come true.

Cirro, again, needed to sound the trumpet to call the group to order. Mother Nature continued to explain, "It seems that the cold-hearted Mrs. Downing has had a change of heart. She is no longer feeding that blanket of warm air with her wounded pride, but has softened her heart to the love of others. She will welcome a beautiful snowfall now."

Amazed and curious, all of the clouds, especially Buff,

questioned her further about the change of events. "We knew the cat was in the barn, but was it finding her that changed Mrs. Downing? She was so angry about her missing cat."

"Oh Buff. You're always so curious. Let's just get these flurries on their way," added Fluff impatiently. "They are really becoming too much to handle now, with all the excitement."

Mother Nature, although firm in her authority, can also be very loving and motherly. "Now, now, everyone, I will be happy to explain. Nature has many ways to warm a heart and heal someone. Sometimes it's a beautiful sunset. Sometimes it's a field of wildflowers. And sometimes, it's a litter of adorable kittens. It seems Miss Bianca has three beautiful kittens to add to Mrs. Downing's household. No one can look at three beautiful kittens without a little warmth in their heart."

"So that is why you were so hopeful, Mother," added Buff. "You knew Bianca was going to have kittens."

"That's right, Buff. Mrs. Downing loves her cat more than anything and with three new kittens to take care of, her life will be that much happier. So now that I have answered your questions, are you bouncing snowflakes ready to fly through the air?"

"I'll lead the way, Mother," answered Denny. "I'm ready to go!"

"Me too," added Crystal. "How do I look? Am I perfectly symmetrical?"

"You are beautiful, Crystal. All of you are," answered Mother Nature. "You make me very proud."

Crystal blushed with the attention. "Thank you, Mother Nature, and I think you are beautiful too."

"Now that we are ready, how does this happen exactly?" asked Stella.

"I will leave the details to Buff and Fluff. I am going back to the Castle of Four Seasons to enjoy it. Have fun!" With that

Mother Nature bade farewell to all and started on her way back to the castle with Cirro and the rest of the cloud guards.

Fluff and Buff watched her leave, grateful for her help, as always. "Mother Nature is so wonderful, isn't she Fluff?"

"She really is," said Fluff misty-eyed.

"Fluff…Buff? Remember us? We are ready to go," called Denny.

With that, Fluff, Buff and all the surrounding clouds instructed the snowflakes to make their way out of their cloud by holding on to one another, with Denny leading the way. Once out of the cloud cover, they could separate and glide gracefully to the ground. "That way, you can come away from the clouds more easily," explained Buff.

As Stella took her place in between Denny and Crystal, she said, "Now we can all go on this adventure together."

"The temperature is just right, everyone. Ready. Set. Go!" exclaimed Fluff. With that, the snowflakes were released from the clouds, swirling and twirling in the wind. The clouds stayed in place, waving goodbye, overjoyed with pride.

"Look Fluff, they are separating, just like we told them to," said Buff with pride.

"I see," answered Fluff. "They are on their way. I think I *already* miss those pesky snowflakes."

Buff looked at Fluff in disbelief. "Are those vapor tears I see? With all your complaints, you're just a softy at heart."

Trying to control himself, Fluff responded, "I am just a little misty-eyed. That's all."

The snowflakes were so overjoyed with their journey to the ground, they didn't even look back at the cloud cover. Their attention was on the village of Silver Slopes below them, with thoughts of all the winter fun they would bring to the villagers.

"Wow! We are finally flying," said Stella. "The village will be even more beautiful when we blanket it in white."

"This is amazing. I'm taking my time gliding down so I can find the perfect place to land," said Crystal.

"I'm having the most fun I've ever had. This is much better than playing in the clouds," added Denny enthusiastically. "Here we come, Silver Slopes. I hope you're ready for us!"

And so the snowflakes made their way toward the unsuspecting village of Silver Slopes. The first snowfall in many, many years.

Chapter 15

SNOWFLAKE MAGIC

*M*ikey sat on the floor of Mrs. Downing's living room in full view of Bianca and her three kittens. He loved watching the kittens, eyes closed, trying to nestle with their mother. Lucy knew it may be difficult to pry Mikey away from them. "Mikey, I think we need to get back to our house. We have all had a very eventful day, and we need to have our supper and a restful night."

"Do we have to go already? I just love watching these kittens."

Mrs. Downing, overjoyed with her new cat family, was touched by the sight of Mikey enjoying them. "Mikey, I will always be grateful to you and Buster for finding Bianca and her kittens. You can come and visit with them whenever you want to, and bring Buster too."

"I can? That's awesome. I think Buster will be best friends with Bianca and the babies from now on. He will probably always protect them."

With that, Mrs. Downing escorted the Doyles to her front door. As they walked out of the house, Mikey looked around and up at the sky in disbelief. "Look, Mrs. Downing, snowflakes! It's snowing!"

With surprise, Mrs. Downing looked up to the sky and saw the sparkling flurries dancing toward the ground. Instead of disappointment, she thought the snow looked enchanting, like a perfect snowflake ballet. "Isn't it beautiful!" Mrs. Downing wondered why she was ever so opposed to something so beautiful. "We can use a little snowfall in Silver Slopes, can't we now?" Mrs. Downing put her arm around his shoulders.

"Yes! And it's going to be awesome!" said Mikey, overjoyed.

Just then, the three pesky snowflakes, Stella, Denny and Crystal began dancing around them, on their way to fulfilling their dreams.

The End

Milton Keynes UK
Ingram Content Group UK Ltd.
UKHW041829310723
426115UK00003B/89